For all those who treasure **Christmas** in their **heart**,
who can hardly wait for the **season** to start!
The ones who know **magic** to be true,
You **believe** in us,
and we believe in **you**.

Love,

Santa & Mrs. Claus

and the elves

Portable North Pole™

Catalogue data available from Bibliothèque
et Archives nationales du Québec

09-17

Printed in Canada

© 2016, UGroupMedia Inc

© 2017, Juniper Publishing,
division of the Sogides Group Inc.,
a subsidiary of Québecor Média Inc.
(Montreal, Quebec)

Originally published by UGroupMedia Inc.
under the title *Twenty-four Sleeps 'til Christmas*

Legal deposit: 2017
National Library of Québec
National Library of Canada

ISBN 978-1-988002-84-2

EXCLUSIVE DISTRIBUTOR:

For Canada:
Simon & Schuster Canada
166 King Street East, Suite 300
Toronto, ON M5A 1J3
phone: (647) 427-8882
       1-800-387-0446
Fax: (647) 430-9446
simonandschuster.ca

Conseil des Arts   Canada Council
du Canada   for the Arts

We gratefully acknowledge the support of the
Canada Council for the Arts for its publishing
program.

We acknowledge the financial support of the
Government of Canada through the Canada Book
Fund for our publishing activities.

Written by Santa Claus

ISBN 978-1-988002-84-2

9 781988 002842

Place your
photo here

My Name

Audrey or audrey

My Age

Where I Live

Welcome to
Santa's Village

Well **hello** there, my friend! I'm glad you stopped by!

I was hoping you'd visit – let me tell you why,

I've lost something **special** – my **magical keys.**

Since you're here in my village, could you help me, please?

The countdown to the **Big Delivery** has begun.

Although we're busy, there's still time for **fun**!

24
SLEEPS
TO GO

Here's a **Craftician** elf – they're always at the ready
To build a doll, a ball, a puzzle or a teddy.
The elves' job isn't to find **magic keys**,
So perhaps you could **help** her, so she can help me?

23 SLEEPS TO GO

Say hello!
They're very gentle but don't be mistaken,
My reindeer won't be stirred up or shaken.
They guide my sleigh by magic and moonbeam,
Presenting this year's fantastic flying team!

22
SLEEPS
TO GO

We **slip** and **slide** on this wintry ride!
When the elves are done working, they **play** outside.

Hush there now and follow me…
We've just arrived at the nursery.
It's Mrs. Claus' greenhouse – see for yourselves,
Enchanted poinsettias tended by Kapunki elves.
The pods will soon blossom and this is from where
Baby elves come from, so – shhhh – you must take care.

20 SLEEPS TO GO

Oopsies!
Postationists! The letters are pouring in!
My **North Pole Post Office** is in a festive tailspin.

19
SLEEPS
TO GO

I have letters to read and notes to write,
And keys to find before the **Big Night!**
I'm learning each child's Christmas wishes,
Mailed to me with **hugs** and **kisses.**
Are you trying your **best?** Are you doing better?
Have you sent your **Santa letter?**

Oh no! We've run out of our **lichen** supply.
Without their **magic** food, my reindeer can't fly.
I sent this **Holhooja** to fetch more moss,
Perhaps she'll find the **key** I've lost?

17
SLEEPS TO GO

Inside, quick! As the chilly **north wind** blows!
We need a **cosy fire** to warm up all our toes.

The elves in the Toy Lab are called Invengineers;
Waving their wands helps them think up new ideas!

We **laugh** at the pranks of the cheeky **Do-Good** elves,
Goodness me, don't they love taking **photos** of themselves?
They swap socks, take snaps and such balderdash.
But **look** closely…a **key** might appear in a flash!

14 SLEEPS TO GO

Oh **dear!** This is such a disappointing surprise...
I checked my **list** and can't believe my eyes!
Too many children being **naughty**, not **nice** –
So you'd better **behave** before I check twice.

13 SLEEPS TO GO

Sometimes we fall down – it happens to us all.
Try to **pick** yourself up and always stand tall.
Be **brave** like the reindeer, **shine** like a Christmas tree!
Show the world your great big **smile** – that's the real key.

12 SLEEPS TO GO

In this room full of **books**, there's one about YOU!
There's a little elf working on it – yes, it's true!
Every child in the world has a special **Big Book**
Filled with all their **news** so I can take a look.

11
SLEEPS
TO GO

The bolts must be **tight** and the rails polished **bright**,
The headlights should glow (to make the magic just right).
I'm fixing my sleigh beneath the **Northern Lights**,
So it **gleams** and **zooms** through the Christmas Eve night.

As **Christmas stars** twinkle and sparkle and brighten,
My reindeer are filling up on **magical lichen**.
Time is flying quickly, everyone agrees,
And I still haven't found all of the missing **keys**!

Christmas crackers, what a **racket**!
Can you **hear** that noise?
Jolly **Crafticians** laugh all day
While they rush to build your **toys**.

8
SLEEPS TO GO

As gentle as a falling snowflake – it's no secret to tell,
True love is so precious in the season of Noel.
Keep your eyes open and go back to the start.
Every step of the way, there's the key to a heart.

Duck for cover!
At the Polar Ranch the **reindeer** train,
While **Holhoojas** play a rollicking game!

6
SLEEPS
TO GO

It **warms** my heart when my workday ends,
To spend some time with my furry **friends**.
Soon I'll be by the fire, in my big comfy chair.
But first, I must find that **key** I left somewhere...

5 SLEEPS TO GO

Cheers! Cheers! Wiggle your ears!
To your **health** and **happiness** for many more jolly years!
All the elves are feeling **festive** as Christmas Day nears.

4
SLEEPS TO GO

At the **tippity-top** of the mountains that
surround our bustling town,
The elves are catching **stardust**, wherever it is found.
Lit by **Northern Lights**, it swirls down all a-glow,
Then they turn it into **golden keys**...
that's a **secret** you should know!

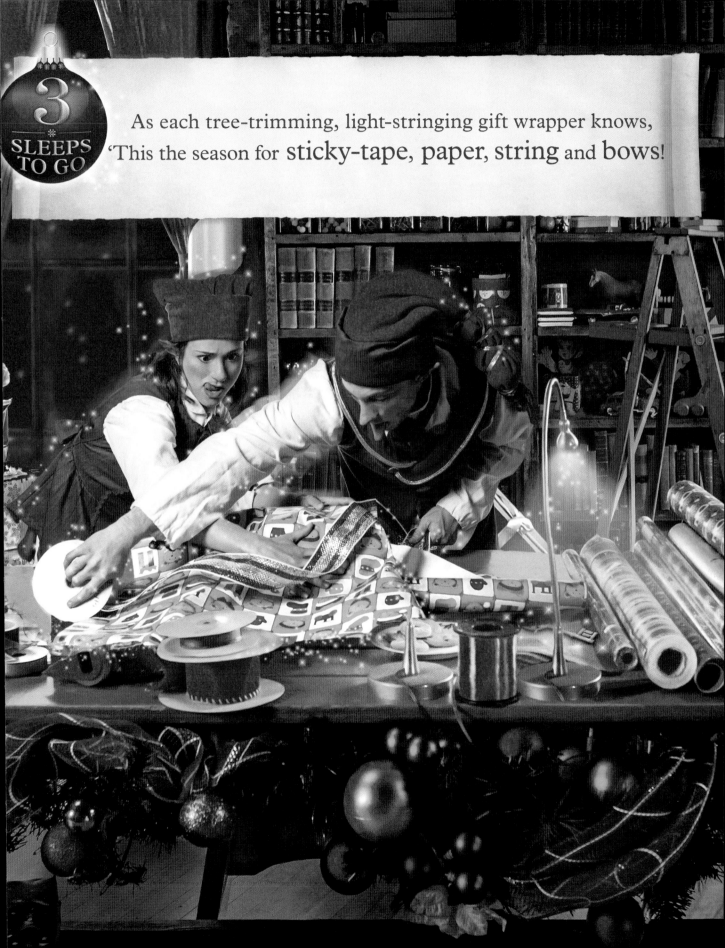

As each tree-trimming, light-stringing gift wrapper knows,
'This the season for **sticky-tape, paper, string** and **bows!**

Santa's Village is a-whirr,
Checking lists and brushing fur.
Counting down, not long to go
'Til I take off with a **"Ho ho ho!"**

01 17 04 59

PNP

1 SLEEP TO GO

My elves are loading the **sleigh**, but I must admit...
With so many **good** children, the gifts might not all fit!
Now the presents are loaded, the sleigh's weighed down
And the reindeer and I are **bound** for your town!
If you hope that I'll visit you, please **don't** make a peep –
Make sure you're tucked up in bed fast **asleep**.

I'm flying to you over **skies** and **seas.**
Thank you for helping us find all of my **keys!**

Merry Christmas!